WELCOME TO THE ANCIENT FAR NORTH... WORLD OF THE M

WHERE THEY LIVE: Miceking Island

CAPITAL: Mouseborg, home of the Stiltonord family

OTHER VILLAGES: Oofadale, village of the Oofa Oofas, and Feargard, village of the vilekings

CLIMATE: Cold, cold, cold, especially when the icy north wind blows!

TYPICAL FOOD: Gloog, a superstinky but fabumouse stew. The secret recipe is closely guarded by the wife of the miceking chief.

NATIONAL DRINK: Finnbrew, made of equal parts codfish juice and herring juice, with a splash of squid ink

MEANS OF TRANSPORTATION: The drekar, a light but very fast ship

GREATEST HONOR: The miceking helmet. It is only earned when a mouse performs an act of courage or wins a Miceking Challenge.

UNIT OF MEASUREMENT: A mouseking tail (full tail, half tail, third tail, quarter tail)

ENEMIES: The terrible dragons who live in Beastgard

MEET THE STILTONORD FAMILY ...

GERONIMO
Advisor to the
miceking chief

THEA
A horse trainer who
works well with all kinds
of animals

TRAP
The most famouse
inventor in Mouseborg

BUGSILDA
Benjamin's best
friend

BENJAMIN
Geronimo's nephew

. . . AND THE EVIL DRAGONS!

GOBBLER THE PUTRID
The fierce king of the dragons is a Devourer!

The dragons are divided into 5 clans, all of which are terrifying!

1. Devourers
They love to eat micekings raw — no cooking necessary.

2. Steamers
They grab micekings, then fly over volcanoes so the steam and smoke make them taste good.

SIZZLE
The cook

3. Biters
Before eating micekings, they nibble them delicately to see if they like them or not.

4. Slurpers
They wrap their long tongues around micekings and slurp them up.

5. Rinsers
As soon as they catch micekings, they rinse them in a stream to wash them off.

Geronimo Stilton

MICEKINGS

THE FAMOUSE FJORD RACE

Scholastic Inc.

Copyright © 2014 by Edizioni Piemme S.p.A., Palazzo Mondadori, Via Mondadori 1, 20090 Segrate, Italy. International Rights © Atlantyca S.p.A. English translation © 2016 by Atlantyca S.p.A.

The publisher does not have any control over and does not assume any responsibility for author or third-party websites or their content.

GERONIMO STILTON names, characters, and related indicia are copyright, trademark, and exclusive license of Atlantyca S.p.A. All rights reserved. The moral right of the author has been asserted. Based on an original idea by Elisabetta Dami. www.geronimostilton.com

Published by Scholastic Inc., *Publishers since 1920*, 557 Broadway, New York, NY 10012. SCHOLASTIC and associated logos are trademarks and/or registered trademarks of Scholastic Inc.

Stilton is the name of a famous English cheese. It is a registered trademark of the Stilton Cheese Makers' Association. For more information, go to www.stiltoncheese.com.

No part of this publication may be reproduced, stored in a retrieval system, or transmitted in any form or by any means, electronic, mechanical, photocopying, recording, or otherwise, without written permission of the copyright holder. For information regarding permission, please contact: Atlantyca S.p.A., Via Leopardi 8, 20123 Milan, Italy; e-mail foreignrights@atlantyca.it, www.atlantyca.com.

ISBN 978-0-545-87239-3

Text by Geronimo Stilton
Original title *Scattare scattareee... Geronimord!*
Cover by Giuseppe Facciotto (pencils) and Flavio Ferron (ink and color)
Illustrations by Giuseppe Facciotto (pencils) and Alessandro Costa (ink and color)
Graphics by Chiara Cebraro

Special thanks to AnnMarie Anderson
Translated by Julia Heim
Interior design by Kay Petronio

10 9 8 7 6 5 4 3 2 1   16 17 18 19 20

Printed in the U.S.A.   40
First printing 2016

GERONIMO,
OUR HERO!

It was a splendid summer afternoon in Mouseborg, the capital of Miceking Island. The sun was **shining** high in the sky, the clouds were rushing past, and a light breeze was making the **flowers** wave in the fields.

Oh, I'm such a **scatterbrain**! I haven't introduced myself: My name is *GERONIMO STILTONORD*, and I am a mouseking. I live in the ancient far north, where it's cold for most of the year — except in the summer! As I was saying, it was a very **HOT** afternoon. It was so hot that I decided to take a little **nap**.

When I woke, I was in the **best mood**. I headed straight toward the town square.  That afternoon the entire village was celebrating a very **special** occasion in honor of *yours truly*. I was about to receive my first **miceking helmet**, our highest honor!

On the street, rodents greeted me with huge smiles and PAWSHAKES. When I arrived in the square, I heard mice cheering my name:

"Geronimo! Our hero has arrived!"

"Cheesy catapults, there he is!"

"It's Geronimo!"

A stage was set up for the ceremony, and it was decorated with crests and C0L0RED flags.

The village chief, SVEN THE SHOUTER, stepped forward and lifted

his arms with a solemn gesture.

All the micekings quieted down.

"**MICEKINGS** of Mouseborg!" Sven exclaimed. "This is a **SPECIAL** day that will be remembered for generations and generations!"

Then he looked my way.

"Come up here, VALIANT Geronimo!" Sven said.

My whiskers **trembling** with emotion, I greeted the crowd and headed for the

stage. Sven the Shouter lifted a **shiny** miceking helmet over my head. Then, in a **thundering** voice, he proclaimed:

"I, Sven the Shouter, award the highest honor to Geronimo the Smarty-mouseking!"

"Hip, hip, hooray!" the crowd answered, shouting as one.

"For his incredible heroism!" Sven shouted.

"Hip, hip, hooray!" everyone replied.

"For his amazing courage!" Sven cried.

"Hip, hip, hooray!" said the crowd.

"And for his fabumouse athletic skills," Sven concluded as he placed the helmet over my snout. "SO SAYS SVEN THE SHOUTER!"

As is customary in Mouseborg, the crowd echoed back:

"SO SAYS SVEN THE SHOUTER!"

I looked out into the audience to see my sister, Thea, my sweet nephew Benjamin, and my cousin Trap **smiling** at me.

Then someone came up behind me and tapped me on the shoulder. I turned to face a mouse with eyes as **blue** as the water of a fjord and hair as **RED** as the sunset.

Helmets and herring! It was **Thora**, Sven's daughter. She is the most courageous and fascinating mouseking in the entire village!

My heart began to pound so loudly I was sure Thora could hear it. As I stared at her **foolishly**, she gave me a **HUG** and **WHiSPeReD**

in my ear: "You look like a true **hero** in that helmet, Geronimo!"

"*Uuuuncle! Uuuuncle!*" a little voice suddenly shrieked loudly.

"H-huh?" I stammered, confused. "Who's that? What's going on?"

"Uncle!" the voice squeaked again.

I opened my eyes and finally understood. The rejoicing crowd . . . my first miceking helmet . . . the courageous Thora: It had all been *just a dream*!

The little voice at my door belonged to my nephew **BENJAMIN**! And that meant I was still at home, half-asleep and in my pajamas.

FJORDS AND FIDDLESTICKS! That also meant I was late for my runes lesson with Benjamin and his friend Bugsilda!

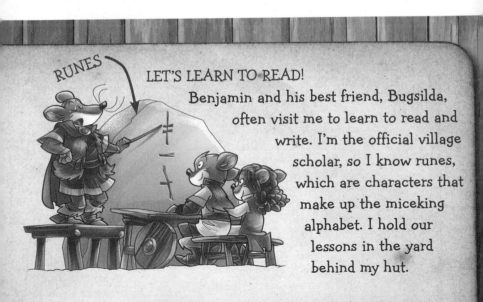

RUNES

LET'S LEARN TO READ!

Benjamin and his best friend, Bugsilda, often visit me to learn to read and write. I'm the official village scholar, so I know runes, which are characters that make up the miceking alphabet. I hold our lessons in the yard behind my hut.

THERE YOU ARE, CODFISH FACE!

I got out of bed and **sighed**. I had only earned a miceking helmet in my dreams. Why, oh why did I have to be the village scholar? I would have traded my brains for brawn in an instant if it meant I could earn my very own **miceking helmet**.

I opened the door to my hut. But before I set one paw outside, I looked up to see if there were any **DRAGONS** in sight. Those **enormouse** creatures are very dangerous because

they're always starved for fresh miceking meat!

Everything seemed calm: The sky was blue, with just a few clouds. So Benjamin, Bugsilda, and I headed to the STONE chalkboard behind my hut. I climbed up onto my stool and began to etch runes into the stone with a PETRIFIED STICK.

"There you are, codfish face!" a voice bellowed.

I recognized that squeak right away. It was Olaf the Fearless, the most obnoxious sea-mouseking and drekar* commander!

"Great groaning glaciers!" I exclaimed. "What are you doing here, Captain?"

"Enough with the chitchat, sailor," Olaf replied. "There's no time to lose! I need your help with a LITTLE JOB. Now get down from that stool and follow me to the port

* A *drekar* is a light but very fast miceking ship.

while there's still a favorable **WIND**!"

Crusty codfish! Just the thought of going out to sea in that little bathtub made my whiskers tremble in **fright**. Anytime I'm on the water, I get terribly **drekar-sick**!

"B-but I have to finish this lesson first," I said, trying to stall. "It's very **IMPORTANT**."

Olaf looked at the stone blackboard.

"Does that explain

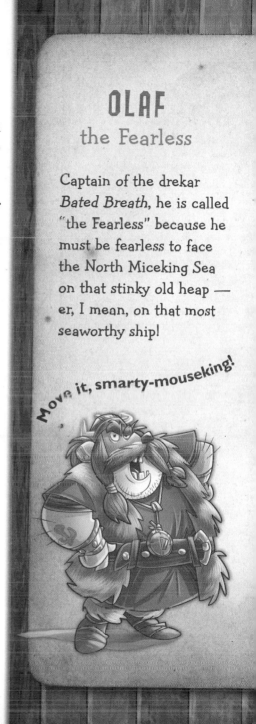

OLAF
the Fearless

Captain of the drekar *Bated Breath*, he is called "the Fearless" because he must be fearless to face the North Miceking Sea on that stinky old heap — er, I mean, on that most seaworthy ship!

Move it, smarty-mouseking!

how to recognize a **TAIL WIND**?"

"No, this is the **ALPHABET**," I replied.

"Well, does it at least explain how to avoid **icebergs** at sea?"

"No," I replied. "It's just the alphabet."

"What about how to use the *stars* to navigate?" he asked. "Or how to tie a miceking knot? Or how to *preserve* herring with salt?"

This is the alphabet . . .

Grrrr!

"No, no, and no!" I answered, exasperated. "It's **still** just the alphabet!"

"Shivering squids!" Olaf yelled. "These lessons are **useless**! When are you going to teach the basic information every good **MOUSEKING SAILOR** needs to know?"

I sighed.

"I don't teach sailing, Olaf," I tried to explain. "I teach reading and writing. Anyway, today's **lesson** is over."

"Great **LESSON**, Uncle G!" Benjamin exclaimed. "Thanks!"

"If you don't mind, can we listen to the **CAPTAIN** now?" Bugsilda added.

Olaf smoothed his **WHISKERS** and smiled.

"You remember my drekar, right?" he said proudly.

"How could I forget that **stinky** — uh, I mean, **BEAUTIFUL** boat?" I replied.

"Well, I'm putting together a team to compete in the **Famouse Fjord Race**, and I need a proper cabin mouse," Olaf explained. "You know, someone who darts back and forth on the deck all day long, **FOLLOWING ORDERS**. Basically, I need someone like you, **SMARTY-MOUSEKING**!"

I need you, smarty-mouseking!

I'M NOT A
SEA-MOUSEKING!

As soon as he heard talk of the **famouse Fjord Race**, Benjamin's ears perked up.

"Yes! Say yes, Uncle!" he shouted. "It's such a barbarically ***fabumouse*** race!"

"And the winner gets a brand-new drekar," Bugsilda added.

"Well said, LITTLE MICEKINGS," Olaf agreed. "The drekar is called *Dame of the Abyss*. She's not as great as *Bated Breath*, but —"

BENJAMIN and **Bugsilda** didn't let him finish.

"A lot of teams will compete," Benjamin squeaked.

"Yeah, it's going to be a **HUGE FIELD**!" Bugsilda cried.

"**Not quite**, little micekings," Olaf corrected. "The course is only for true sea-micekings who are willing to **risk their fur**. It's not going to be easy!"

I sighed with relief. This was my **OUT**!

"I'm not a true sea-mouseking!" I cried. "So I'm afraid I can't be your cabin mouse, Olaf."

But Olaf just gave me an enormouse **THUMP** on the back.

"Unfortunately, the best **SAILORS** are all busy," Olaf replied. "You're the only one left, **smarty-mouseking**. But don't worry: You're as weak as a baby herring now, but you won't be for long. On the honor of Olaf the Fearless!"

"B-but, I can't leave!" I protested. "I have too many things to do in Mouseborg."

"Oh, yeah?" Olaf asked, looking me up and down. "And what exactly do you have to do that's so **URGENT**?"

"Umm . . . I have to dust the attic and **SHARPEN** the petrified sticks for sketching runes," I squeaked meekly.

"No more excuses!" the commander burst out. "Don't be a **BONELESS COD**. It's up to you, smarty-mouseking. Now get ready to go — captain's orders!"

I tried one more time.

"Oh, you don't understand, Captain," I moaned. "All this **sun** is going to give me a furburn. And I suffer from the **WORST** drekar-sickness!"

"Stop complaining!" Olaf grunted. "You're leaving with me, and that's that!"

I sighed. It was **IMPOSSIBLE** to change his mind.

At that moment, my sister, **THEA**, rode up proudly on her white horse. She's a horse trainer with a real gift for working with animals.

"Your brother is as **soft** as a fish fillet!" Olaf complained to her. "He keeps inventing **EXCUSES** so he won't have to participate in the race. It's just as I suspected!"

Thea looked me over with a **stern** expression.

"*GERONIMO STILTONORD!*" she scolded. "I assured the commander that you would be a part of his crew. It's the **perfect** excuse for you to put those petrified sticks aside and get some **sun** and **exercise**!"

Stop complaining!

He's as soft as a fish fillet!

Huff!

When I say no, I mean no!

"Thea's **RIGHT**!" Olaf exclaimed.

I couldn't believe my ears: These two had **TEAMED UP**!

"When I say no, I mean no," I said stubbornly.

"Think about it, Geronimo," **THEA** suggested. "Instead of **WRITING** about the heroic actions of other micekings, you could write about your **own adventures** for once."

I was about to dig in my paws and refuse when Benjamin and Bugsilda joined in.

"Uncle, it will be a fabumouse race!" Benjamin squeaked.

"We'll all participate **together**," Bugsilda added.

At that point I didn't have any **MORE**

excuses — I would do anything to make my sweet little nephew and his friend **happy**. I sat down on my stool and sighed.

"Okay," I agreed. "We'll take part in the race."

"Yaaaay!" Benjamin rejoiced.

Olaf and **THEA** winked at each other. Their plan had worked!

Olaf gave me another heavy **paw** to the back.

"That's the spirit, smarty-mouseking!" he said. "We depart tomorrow morning. Be at the port at ***dawn***!"

THE FAMOUSE FJORD RACE

The next morning when I arrived at the port, everything was ready for the start of the **Famouse Fjord Race**.

The drekar captains had their boats lined up at the start. Crowds of micekings packed the docks, CHEERING for their favorite boats.

Sven the Shouter had ordered a **superduper**,

Goat-butter-and-fjordberry-jam sandwiches

Aged Stenchberg cheese on toast

Mousehilde's famouse gloog

extra-long table for the occasion. It was loaded with a ton of whisker-licking-good food!

All the most appetizing **mouseking** specialties were there:

- Goat-butter-and-**fjordberry-jam** sandwiches
- Aged **Stenchberg** cheese on toast
- Famouse **gloog** stew made by Sven's wife, Mousehilde
- **Seaweed** spaghetti with goat cheese
- Assorted **MUSSELS**
- **Salted-codfish** ice cream

Seaweed spaghetti with goat cheese

Assorted mussels

Salted-codfish ice cream

I had just arrived when **SVEN THE SHOUTER** made an announcement at the top of his lungs.

"Micekings of Mouseborg, rejoice!" he cried. "The **Famouse Fjord Race** is about to begin!"

All the micekings on the docks replied: "Yip! Yip! Yippeee!"

"Fearless **sea** rodents, I know you'll all behave like true sportsmice," Sven continued. "May the best team win. **SO SAYS SVEN THE SHOUTER!**"

All the micekings on the docks replied: **"SO SAYS SVEN THE SHOUTER!"**

Then Sven spotted me.

"Geronimo, you're just getting here **NOW**?" he thundered. "Also, you look a bit greenish!"

"Valiant Sven the Shouter, I have to admit something," I said, my cheeks turning

RED with embarrassment. "I have a bit of a stomachache. Y-you know, I s-suffer from **terrible drekar-sickness!**"

Sven sighed.

"You really are a boneless cod, smarty-mouseking," he said, shaking his head. "Now, get your tail on the *Bated Breath* and act like a true mouscking. **SO SAYS SVEN THE SHOUTER!**"

The micekings on the docks all shouted in unison: **"SO SAYS SVEN THE SHOUTER!"**

I **sighed** in resignation and headed toward Olaf's boat.

At that moment, a voice behind me made me **JUMP**.

"Heya, Cuz!"

"Trap!" I cried. "Are you on **Olaf the Fearless's** crew, too?"

"Of course not!" Trap replied. "But I heard

you're participating in the race, so I brought you a **GIFT**!"

Fjords and fiddlesticks! I was in trouble. When my cousin Trap has a gift for me, it means one of two things: He needs a favor or he wants me to test out one of his latest inventions. And his inventions **NEVER**, **EVER** work!

He pointed to what looked like a simple WOODEN barrel.

"This is a **DANGEROUS** race, Cousin," he said. "And since you're a real **CODFISH**, I know that sooner or later, you're going to fall in the water. So you can test out my new invention: the Emergency Lifeboat in a Barrel!"

"No, no, no!" I shouted. "You know I don't like your inventions!"

"This isn't like my other inventions," Trap

reasoned. "It's supereasy to use. You don't even need instructions! When you get back to **MOUSEBORG** — that is, *if* you get back — you'll **thank me**!"

With that, he **PUSHED** the mysterious **barrel** toward me.

Resigned, I headed to the buffet and helped myself to a double serving of Mousehilde's gloog with a side of **salted-codfish**

THE EMERGENCY LIFEBOAT IN A BARREL

For the mouseking who doesn't know how to swim! This invention is ideal for keeping micekings afloat and protecting their tails from sharks. Steering accessories (paddles and oars) are strictly excluded. Portable, spacious, and so easy to use that there are no instructions!

It's quite an invention!

ice cream. After all, who knew when I'd eat again!

Good-bye, **miceking banquets**! Good-bye, fur! Good-bye, lovely **Thora**!

Who knows when I'll eat again!

MICEKING CHALLENGE!

I was still cating when a **TALL**, **MUSCULAR** rodent approached.

"Do you plan on serving me some ice cream or not?" she asked. "A cabin mouse must do his **DUTY**, even on dry land!"

"B-but I-I'm not really a c-c-cabin mouse," I **stuttered**. "And I'm n-not serving ice cream . . ."

At that moment, **Thora** arrived.

"I didn't know you were participating in the race, too, Geronimo," she said. "Let me introduce Ratilde, the captain of the *Beauty of the Seas*!"

I extended a paw to the tall, muscular rodent, and she gave it a vigorous shake.

RATILDE

Ratilde is the captain of the drekar *Beauty of the Seas*. Her fabumouse all-female crew is one of the best in Mouseborg. But don't be fooled by her friendliness: Ratilde can challenge and defeat any sea-mouseking!

My drekar is the best!

"Captain Ratilde, this is GERONIMO, my dad's advisor and the village **scholar**," Thora explained.

I couldn't believe my ears: The most **fascinating** rodent in the village was talking about ME! I was about to melt like Stenchberg cheese in the sun. Ratilde introduced me to the courageous **micekings** who made up the *Beauty of the Seas* crew.

Unable to avoid my

cabin-mouse duties, I served ice cream to everyone on the dock with a smile on my snout.

But suddenly, Olaf **arrived**, shouting at me.

"Geronimo, does this seem like the time to eat ice cream?" he asked, annoyed. "Get on board, you **JELLYFISH**!"

"Olaf, you **SEA RAT**!" Ratilde greeted him. "Did you forget how to greet an old friend?"

As soon as he saw her, Olaf turned as **RED** as a shrimp. I had never seen him so embarrassed!

"R-Ratilde!" he stammered. "I-I didn't s-see you there! Pardon me. You know, preparations for the **RACE** are keeping me **busy**. And speaking of the race, may the best team win!"

SNARL

The commander of the *Cyclone Prince*, the drekar with the most muscly mickings in Mouseborg. He is famouse because he snarls constantly, especially when Olaf the Fearless is nearby.

Grrrr, I'm the best!

"In that case, you might as well quit right now!" SNICKERED a supermuscular rodent with a BRAIDED beard. "Ha, ha, ha!"

It was Snarl, the COMMANDER of the *Cyclone Prince*, the drekar with the tallest and beefiest miceking crew in all of Mouseborg.

"Go ahead and stay there eating ice cream," he continued. "My drekar will definitely win the race!"

"Oh, **great groaning glaciers**!" Olaf thundered, furious. "A true sea-mouseking doesn't eat ice cream!"

"Oh, really?" Ratilde jumped in. "I **ADORE** ice cream!"

Olaf was silent in embarrassment.

Ratilde had a **weakness** for ice cream, but Olaf didn't know about it until now. For that matter, Olaf had a **weakness** for Ratilde, but she didn't know about it at all!

Snarl took the opportunity to try to make Olaf **jealous**.

"We **UNDERSTAND** each other completely, Ratilde!" he said. "I **ADORE** ice cream, too. I can eat an entire barrelful, unlike this jellyfish, Olaf!"

Hearing those words, all the micekings began to chant:

"MICEKING CHALLENGE! MICEKING CHALLENGE! MICEKING CHALLENGE!"

Olaf turned to look me right in the eye.

"I will eat more **ice cream** than Snarl," he said confidently. *"On the honor of Olaf the Fearless!* Geronimo, since you are a scholar, you will be our judge and referee."

Cheesy catapults! Not a Miceking Challenge! Every time I'm asked to judge a Miceking Challenge, I end up in **TROUBLE**. And in this case, in addition to being the judge, I'd have to serve the **ice cream**! But the micekings around me continued to chant:

"MICEKING CHALLENGE! MICEKING CHALLENGE! MICEKING CHALLENGE!"

In the end, I had to do it.

"**READY?**" I announced. "On your marks, get set . . . **go**!"

And the Miceking Challenge began!

Olaf and Snarl **gobbled down** one bowl of **salted-codfish** ice cream after the next. One, two, three . . . ten, eleven, twelve . . . twenty, twenty-one, twenty-two bowls of ice cream! They were **TIED** until there was just one bowl left. At that point, I didn't know whom to serve *FIRST*!

"Give me that ice cream, you **codfish face!**" Olaf thundered.

Oops!

"No, give it to me!" Snarl growled. "Grrr!"

So I held it in my paws without deciding. But the two drekar captains *yanked* me, **PULLED** me, and spun me around as they tried to get the ice cream!

In the end, the bowl slipped out of my paws, flew into the air, and landed right on my snout!

"Squeak!" I cried.

For a moment, Olaf and Snarl **STARED** at me in silence. Then the questions began:

"So who ate more ice cream?"

"Yeah, who's the winner?"

"You decide, SMARTY-MOUSEKING!"

All the other micekings who had watched

the challenge started to yell at me, too.

"Come on, smarty-mouseking!" they chanted. "**Hurry up** and pick a winner!"

Olaf and Snarl were about to start **yanking** me again, but right at that moment, **Stocker** the warehouse worker arrived.

"Valiant Sven the Shouter," he yelled at the top of his lungs. "The finnbrew is **MISSING**!"

Finnbrew is the national miceking beverage. It is made from fish that are blended, spun, filtered, and poured into wooden barrels. Then it is macerated in the sun until it is covered in a layer of flies and fermented to perfection! The ingredients are codfish juice, herring juice, and a splash of squid ink.

They Stole the Finnbrew!

As soon as he saw the rodent **running** along the dock, Sven made space in the crowd.

"What happened?" Sven asked.

"There's no more **finnbrew**, valiant Sven the Shouter!" Stocker repeated, panting.

"**WHAAAAT?!**" Sven thundered. "Where has it gone?"

"I don't know," Stocker replied with a shrug.

"Then it must have been STOLEN!" said Sven's wife, Mousehilde.

"Stolen?" Stocker asked, confused. "Well, er, yes, maybe . . . or not . . ."

Sven, Mousehilde, and I exchanged glances. Everyone in Mouseborg knows that Stocker is always indecisive. If you're in a **HURRY**, it's better not to ask him too many questions!

Sven turned **RED** with anger.

"Whatever happened to it, we **must** find it!" he shouted. "In the meantime, sailors, prepare to depart! The race must go on!"

Then Sven grabbed my arm.

"Come on, Geronimo," he **SAID**. "You're **INTELLIGENT**! I need your help."

We crossed the port

STOCKER

Stocker works in the warehouse at the finnbrew factory in Mouseborg. His job is to organize, watch, and deliver the barrels of finnbrew. He is a very indecisive mouseking. When you ask him a question, he'll usually just stare at you like a frozen codfish!

in a **flash** and entered the finnbrew warehouse.

"It's as empty as the belly of a bear after a long winter hibernating!" Sven thundered.

"The only thing left is this TRUNK for the brewing equipment," Stocker

pointed out. "But it's EMPTY, too."

"When did this happen?" Mousehilde asked him.

"I checked the finnbrew **BarreLS** for the race yesterday and everything was in order," Stocker said. "At least I THINK it was in order . . ."

"It's all your fault, Sven!" Mousehilde shouted at her husband. "I told you we needed to put a **security mouseking** in here!"

"But something doesn't add up," I said thoughtfully as I looked around. "How did the thief take all the **finnbrew**? And where is it now?"

Stocker showed me the **key** around his neck.

"It's true," he explained. "There's only one entrance to the cellar . . . I think. And I have the only key!"

SECURITY MOUSEKING

Yaaawn!

This mouseking watches houses and warehouses twenty-four hours a day. He begins to yell like a barbarian anytime someone unauthorized approaches. You can recognize him by the multilayered bags under his eyes. Be careful: He is very irritable, grouchy, and moody because he never gets any sleep!

"Hmmm," I mused. "This is all **very, very strange**."

"That's enough **INVESTIGATING** for now," Sven decided as he dragged me back to the port by my whiskers. "You can figure it out after the **RACE**, scholar! **SO SAYS SVEN THE SHOUTER!**"

When we returned to the docks, a great wind had picked up. All the teams were at the **STARTING LINE**.

Thea poked her head out of the *Bated Breath*.

"Hurry, Geronimo!" she squeaked.

"Come on, Uncle!" Benjamin cried. "We've been waiting for you!"

I climbed aboard to find Captain Olaf on the deck, clutching his stomach.

"**OH, OH, OH!**" he moaned. "What a **stomachache!**"

"Do you feel okay, Captain?" I asked, concerned. "Your snout is **greener** than mine."

"It's all that **salted-codfish** ice cream!" Olaf replied. "I ate too much! *Ooooh, I feel so sick!*"

"Does that mean we're not going to leave?" I asked hopefully. "We're going to *quit the race*, right?"

"No!" he replied firmly. "A true sea rodent **NEVER** gives

Get moving!

I have to steer it?!

up. You'll have to steer the drekar, Geronimo!"

ME?!

Olaf showed me to the helm of the ship.

"Cast off and adjust the sheets, **smarty-mouseking**," he ordered. "Then hoist the sails and tack to portside!"

Having said that, the captain DISAPPEARED belowdecks.

SHiVERiNG SQUiDS!

I was in charge, and I hadn't **understood** a thing!

DICTIONARY OF NAUTICAL TERMS

LINE: Rope

CAST OFF: Release the ropes; set sail

SHEET: The rope that lets you adjust a sail

ADJUST THE SHEETS: Pull the ropes that control the sails

HOIST THE SAILS: Raise the sails

PORT: The left side of the boat

STARBOARD: The right side of the boat

I always have to explain everything!

Ready . . .
Set . . . Go!

On the shore, Sven positioned himself in front of a beautiful new drekar.

"Micekings, turn your snouts toward the *Dame of the Abyss*," he announced. "This jewel of a ship will be presented to the **winner** of the race!"

Dame of
the Abyss

"**OOOOOH!**" the crowd murmured.

I was still busy trying to understand what I had to do. Had Olaf told me to **cast off**? And did he say something about **SHEETS**?! But what did it mean to cast off? And what was a sheet? **Crusty codfish!** I didn't have a **CLUE**!

Meanwhile, Sven was announcing the rules of the race.

"The first team to reach the **WHISKERED ROCK**, take the *flag*, and return to the port will win the **Famouse Fjord Race**!" he bellowed.

"Hooray!" shouted the spectators.

"Take your places!" Sven thundered. "Ready . . . set . . . go!"

All the drekars **DARTED** forward, fighting to be the first to leave the port. Every drekar . . . except ours!

THE TEAMS COMPETING IN THE FAMOUSE FJORD RACE

CAPTAIN: Olaf the Fearless

CHARACTERISTICS Proud and headstrong sea-mouseking with long red whiskers

DREKAR NAME: *Bated Breath* (because it could sink at any moment!)

CREW: The Stiltonord family (except for Trap, who was too busy!) and little Bugsilda

CAPTAIN: Ratilde
CHARACTERISTICS: Fascinating and bold sea-mouseking
DREKAR NAME: *Beauty of the Seas* (because of the splendid siren on its bow!)
CREW: The gutsiest female micekings in the ancient far north (including Thora)

CAPTAIN:
Snarl
CHARACTERISTICS: Beefy and
sly sea-mouseking with a braided beard
DREKAR NAME: *Cyclone Prince* (because it crushes
anything in its path!)
CREW: The tallest and beefiest micekings in Mouseborg

"Why aren't we **MOVING**, Geronimo?" Thea asked impatiently.

"Umm . . . I-I don't know!" I said. "I'm definitely not a sea-mouseking!"

But Benjamin and Bugsilda urged me on.

"Don't get **DISCOURAGED**, Uncle!" Benjamin squeaked encouragingly. "We know you can do it!"

The little micekings were right. I could do it! I had to do it!

I went over Olaf's instructions again.

Cast off: Done! (Well, okay, Benjamin did it!)

Adjust the sheets: Done! (I'm not sure what they are, but Thea took care of it!)

Hoist the sails: Done! (Bugsilda did it!)

Tack to portside: This I could do . . . or at least I thought I could!

I tried, but the drekar turned uselessly from

one side to the **other**!

Why, why, why couldn't I **figure** this out? The wind was favorable, the sails were full . . . What had I forgotten?

Meanwhile, Benjamin and Bugsilda darted up and down the deck, trying to help.

"Uncle, the anchor!" Benjamin shouted.

SHIVERING SQUIDS! The anchor was keeping us in place!

Without wasting any more time, I raised the anchor, and *Bated Breath* darted forward. I tried to tack, but instead of me **turning** the rudder, the rudder was turning me! So the drekar spun around on itself in the middle of the port, causing the micekings on the shore to **crack up** laughing.

As the boat started spinning, I began to get **DreKar-sicK**!

"Quit playing the fool and get going, smarty-mouseking!" Sven shouted from shore. **"SO SAYS SVEN THE SHOUTER!"**

And from the dock, everyone squeaked together: **"SO SAYS SVEN THE SHOUTER!"**

Luckily, right at that moment, **Olaf** returned to the deck, grabbed the rudder, and took matters into his own paws. He **straightened out** the *Bated Breath* right away!

"C-captain, th-thank GOODNESS you've come back!" I **stammered**. "H-how did you manage to get better so **QUICKLY?**"

"True sea rodents know a **SUREFIRE** method to cure stomachaches in the flick of a whisker!" he said cryptically. "But I have no time to explain right now. At your posts! **We're off!**"

Olaf the Fearless was a real mouseking sailor. He had **rallied** big-time! The race had begun, and we were **on our way** at last!

THE GULF OF FLOATING ISLANDS

We were sailing in the open **sea** under the hot sun when we saw the Gulf of Floating Islands. In the distance, we **GLIMPSED** the *Cyclone Prince* zigzagging between the islands, with a few tails' advantage over the *Beauty of the Seas*.

"Look, Uncle!" Benjamin exclaimed. "The islands are moving!"

"No," I replied. "Islands **can't** move."

But then I saw them move myself!

I shook my snout. **Huh?**

"It must be a trick of the light," I said, perplexed. "But it actually does seem like

everything is **moving** . . .”

"Maybe that's why they're called floating islands," Bugsilda suggested.

"But if that's the case, what happens if one of the islands *bumps into* the drekar when we sail by?" I asked, worried.

Olaf was not reassuring.

"Simple," he replied. "Then the drekar will sink, and we'll become **shark bait**!”

Great groaning glaciers! My whiskers trembled with fright.

Shark bait?!

"Don't be scared, Uncle," Benjamin said calmly. **"Captain Olaf** is the best navigator there is!"

Meanwhile, the other teams

doused their sails (in other words, they lowered their sails and **SLOWED DOWN**!) and carefully navigated between the islands.

"Have you seen the other drekars?" Thea asked. "It's no problem. There's nothing to worry about."

But I was worried. We were getting **closer** and **closer** to the islands, but Olaf didn't seem to be **SLOWING DOWN** at all!

"Um, Captain?" I asked meekly. "Wouldn't it be better to DOUSE THE SAILS a bit?"

"There's no time to slow down," he replied boldly. "We need to make up for our delay. We'll tackle those islands at *FULL SPEED*!"

At f-full s-speed?

SHIVERING SQUIDS!

"With this TAIL WIND, we'll reach the *Cyclone Prince* in the swish of a tail!" Olaf cried confidently.

At that moment, the drekar jolted violently. I lost my balance and tripped over a coil of rope. [1]

My paw got caught in the rope, and a second jolt hoisted me up into the air, where I dangled upside down by one paw. Yikes! [2]

Look out!

Ack!

1

2

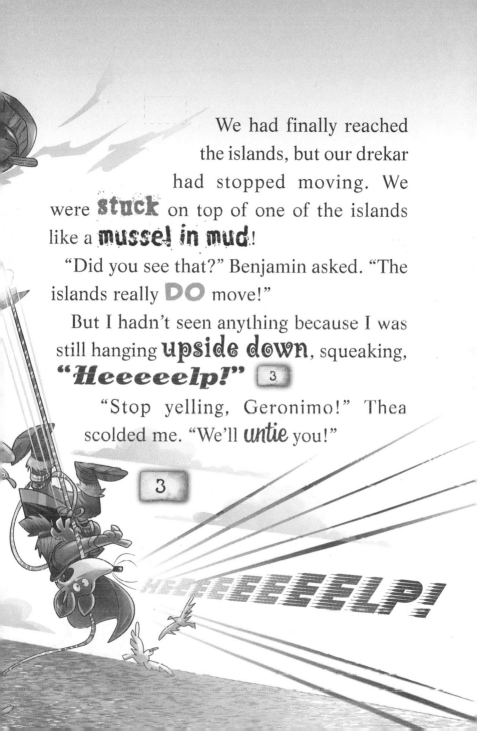

We had finally reached the islands, but our drekar had stopped moving. We were **stuck** on top of one of the islands like a **mussel in mud**!

"Did you see that?" Benjamin asked. "The islands really **DO** move!"

But I hadn't seen anything because I was still hanging **upside down**, squeaking, **"Heeeeelp!"** 3

"Stop yelling, Geronimo!" Thea scolded me. "We'll **untie** you!"

3

From where I was hanging, I suddenly did see something, and it wasn't good. The island we were stuck on was FLOODING with water! It happened slowly at first, but then *faster* and *FASTER*. I couldn't believe my eyes: The islands actually weren't islands! They were enormouse fin whales whose rough skin had become **encrusted** with earth. Palm trees had even sprouted on the whales' backs!

It looked like the island we were stuck on was

flooding because the whale had started to sound.

"**HELP!**" I continued to shout. "Get me down!"

Fortunately, Benjamin was finally able to **LOOSEN** the rope.

Unfortunately, I fell **STRAIGHT** down onto the deck, landing right on my tail! **Ouchie!**

"Quit wasting time, codfish face!" Olaf growled at me. "We're in the middle of a race. We have to figure out how to get **OFF** this whale!"

"Leave it to me," Thea said confidently.

Then she leaned over the side of the drekar to get **closer** to the whale. My sister has the **unique** ability to talk to animals, which was what she was doing now.

A moment later, Thea turned to us with a **smile**.

"We have an idea!" she said. "Hold on tight, everyone!"

"What?!" I exclaimed. "You're not thinking of . . . **NOOOOO!**"

At that moment, the whale began to **SPRAY** a super-strong stream of water from its blowhole. **SPLASH!**

The stream was so strong that it **shot** us into the air and **CATAPULTED** us to the other side of the Gulf of **Floating Islands**!

We're catching up!

THE WHISKERED ROCK

We landed a few tail-lengths from the ***Beauty of the Seas***.

But we were still in last place!

The *Cyclone Prince*, meanwhile, had already arrived at the Whiskered Rock. **BENJAMIN** and *Bugsilda* were as curious as cats about the famouse rock. They began to bombard Olaf with questions:

"**1 – Why** does the rock look like a mouseking with a fish's tail?

· "**2 – Why** do they say the rock is 'whiskered'?

"**3 – Why** is the *Cyclone Prince* so close to the rock?"

The commander responded to each question:

"1 – I don't know! It's a mystery.

"2 – Because a colony of blue walruses lives there.

"3 – Because Snarl wants to grab the flag without docking, which isn't sportsmouselike at all! That **COD FACE**!"

The *Cyclone Prince* went around the Whiskered Rock, passing **VERY**, **VERY** close to the flags. Snarl grabbed one, and his drekar took off!

The *Cyclone Prince* passed right by us.

Blue Walrus

True sea rodents say that this large, heavy sea mammal is the reason the landmark is called the Whiskered Rock. It eats shellfish, shellfish, and more shellfish but has been rumored to eat mickings when angry. Blue walruses have never-ending appetites, but they get terrible stomachaches when they eat too much!

"Olaf, you old sea rat!" Snarl snarled. "I grabbed that flag right out from under your snout! If you're nice, I'll let you take a little spin in my new drekar, the *Dame of the Abyss*. HA, HA, HA!"

"That's no way to behave!" Olaf huffed.

But our **troubles** were just beginning. While SNARL was distracting Olaf, the blue walruses had surrounded the *Bated Breath* and the *Beauty of the Seas* threateningly!

"It's all Snarl's fault!" Ratilde shouted from her drekar. "He must have disturbed them when he sailed too close to the rock. Now they're **furious**!"

The entire colony of blue walruses was ready to BITE into the first micekings that passed by — in other words, us! Even worse, there was NO WAY for us to get close to the flags without passing them.

Suddenly, we were startled by a loud sound: **Buuuurp!**

"Come on, Geronimo," Olaf exclaimed. "You could at least excuse yourself!"

Buuuurp!

"What?" I replied, confused. "That wasn't me! Was it you, Thea?"

Buuuurp!

"No, it wasn't me," Thea replied as she climbed down from a Rope ladder. "It was the blue walruses! I'll go check it out."

"Be careful where you put your paws, Auntie," Benjamin warned. "The rock is covered in SHARP shells!"

But it was **no problem** for my sister. She's such a **COURAGEOUS** mouseking! She approached the blue walruses slowly and carefully, talking to them **softly** the entire time. Then she turned back to us.

"I understand why they're **burping**!" she exclaimed. "They have **stomachaches** from eating too many **SHELLFISH**!"

"So they don't want to *attack* us?" I asked.

I come in peace!

"No," Thea replied, shaking her head.

"But how can we **HELP** them?" Benjamin asked.

"I know!" Olaf said, **smoothing** his whiskers. "I have an 𝕀ℕ𝔽𝔸𝕃𝕃𝕀𝔹𝕃𝔼 cure for stomachaches!"

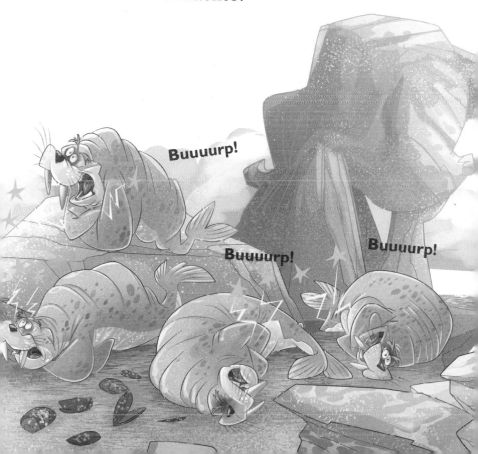

Buuuurp!

Buuuurp!

Buuuurp!

DON'T BE A
SHRIMP HEAD!

Captain Olaf disappeared belowdecks and returned holding a **root** with green leaves in his paw.

"What is that?" I asked.

"I thought you were a smarty-mouseking!" Olaf teased. "This root is the **REMEDY** I used for the stomachache I got from eating that salted-codfish ice cream! It's called **RATUZEN ROOT**."

RATUZEN ROOT

This root can be found on a remote island in the extreme far north. Only the most courageous sea-micekings know how to get there!

"**HOORAY!**" Benjamin and Bugsilda rejoiced. "It will make the blue walruses' **stomachaches** go away!"

"You can bet on it!" Olaf agreed. "True sea rodents have **PASSED DOWN** this remedy from one miceking generation to the next since the **dawn** of time. Eating a bit of it will make a stomachache pass *quickly*."

Thea gave a slice of the **ROOT** to each of the walruses. As their stomachaches passed, they began to howl in **joy**, celebrating with clumsy jumps.

But above all, they cleared the path so that our crew could get to the **flags**!

Unfortunately, the *Beauty of the Seas* had been damaged during its approach by the **POINTY** edges of the Whiskered Rock.

"We can't continue the race," Ratilde

concluded after she **EXAMINED** her drekar. "But you go ahead, Olaf. We'll make do!"

"No way," Olaf replied. "I, **Olaf the Fearless**, am a mouseking of honor. We won't leave you here!"

Don't worry, we'll be okay!

We'll help you!

"Don't be a shrimp head, Olaf!" Ratilde insisted. "That crusty old codfish Snarl doesn't deserve to win. Leave us and head for the finish. The best thing you can do for the *Beauty of the Seas* is to beat the *Cyclone Prince!*"

Wow! What a determined mouseking!

Olaf saw the logic of Ratilde's argument. Ratilde and her crew stayed behind to repair the *Beauty of the Seas* as we continued the race.

After a few minutes, though, we found ourselves in the middle of an ENORMOUSE storm. Captain Olaf called out orders LEFT and right, barely pausing for a breath.

"Get moving, Geronimo! Cast off, Geronimo! Row, Geronimo, rooooooow!"

But all I could do was slip and fall on the deck, which was WET from the waves.

I felt so **drekar-sick**, I thought I might **toss my cheese**!

"Come on, Geronimo," Olaf thundered. "When we make it to the finish line you won't be a **barnacle** anymore — you'll be a real **sailor**! Now climb that main mast and let

Gulp!

me know how **FAR** we are from Snarl's drekar!"

So I climbed to the top of the main mast . . .

Crusty codfish! It was really, really high up!

I don't just get drekar-sick; I'm afraid of **HEIGHTS**, too! From the top of the mast, I could see that the *wind* had pushed us so hard we had cut into the *Cyclone Prince*'s lead. We were 𝕹𝔼ℂ𝕂 and 𝕹𝔼ℂ𝕂 with Snarl's drekar!

"Give up, fluke face!" Snarl yelled.

"Out of our way, sea rat!" Olaf countered.

Our drekars were so close, they kept colliding! A strong *jolt* threw me from the main mast right into the sea.

MOUSEKING
OVERBOARD!

Luckily, Thea noticed my fall.

"**MOUSEKING OVERBOAAARD!**" she yelled.

I flapped my paws, my tail, and my whiskers around in a **DESPERATE** attempt to stay afloat, but I'm not a very **ATHLETIC** mouseking. In fact, I can barely **SWIM**!

"There's no time to lose!" Olaf shouted as he turned the drekar around to get me. The *Cyclone Prince* took advantage of our misfortune and **DARTED** toward the finish line without even pausing to help. In fact, Snarl **laughed** as he sped by.

"See you at the awards ceremony, **seaweed breath**!" he snarled. "**HA, HA, HA!**"

At that moment, a group of fins popped out of the water and began CIRCLING me.

"Blasted barnacles!" Olaf yelled. "There are SHARKS!"

"HELP!" I shouted. "I'm shark bait!"

"I have an idea," Benjamin squeaked. "Aunt Thea, this would be a great time to test out Trap's Emergency Lifeboat in a Barrel!"

I sighed. Not Trap's invention! His ideas never, EVER seemed to work!

Meanwhile, more sharks were approaching.

Heeeeelp!

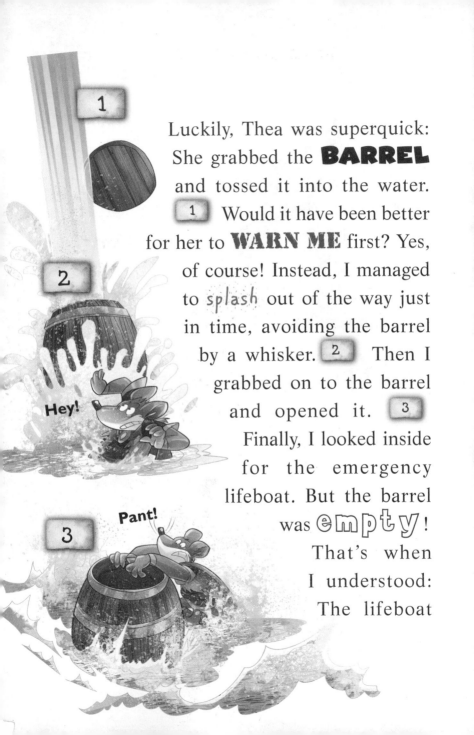

1

Luckily, Thea was superquick: She grabbed the **BARREL** and tossed it into the water. **1** Would it have been better for her to **WARN ME** first? Yes, of course! Instead, I managed to *splash* out of the way just in time, avoiding the barrel by a whisker. **2** Then I grabbed on to the barrel and opened it. **3** Finally, I looked inside for the emergency lifeboat. But the barrel was ⓔⓜⓟⓣⓨ! That's when I understood: The lifeboat

2

Hey!

3

Pant!

wasn't INSIDE the barrel — the lifeboat *was* the barrel!

I **pulled myself** into the barrel and tried to figure out how it worked. But there was nothing to *figure out*. All the barrel did was float!

"Hooray!" Benjamin yelled happily. "It works! Uncle Trap said it was easy to use."

But Thea still looked worried.

"Careful, Geronimo!" she shouted, pointing at the circle of fins that was moving closer and closer to me.

I ducked down inside the barrel, my

Now what?

whiskers trembling in fright. Something bumped the outside of my lifeboat.

Shivering squids! I was sure I was about to lose my fur. I peeked over the edge of the barrel and found myself snout-to-snout with . . . a dolphin. I wasn't surrounded by SHARKS — they were DOLPHiNS! Whew!

The friendly creatures began to **playfully** toss the barrel back and forth.

BOING! BOING! BOING!

Helmets and herring! I was soaking wet and my head was **spinning**, but I was safe!

Benjamin and Bugsilda laughed with relief. Thea **thanked** the dolphins, petting their snouts.

But our good mood was cut short by the **terrifying** sound of a horn:

TOOT, TOOT, TOOOOOOT!

"Dragon alert!" Olaf shouted.

What a headache!

Boing!

RATNOLF THE TERRIBLE

A dolphin tossed me onto the deck of the *Bated Breath* with a flip of his tail, then the pod quickly dispersed in the clear waters of the fjord.

"D-dragons!" I stuttered in fear. "Wh-where?"

We all **looked up**, but there was nothing in the sky.

"I don't see anything," Thea said hopefully. "Maybe it was a **FALSE** alarm . . ."

But a moment later we spotted a mysterious drekar with a **DARK** flag waving from its mast.

"**SHIVERING SQUIDS!**" Olaf exclaimed. "It's the **VILEKINGS**!"

I shuddered. The vilekings are the most

TROUBLESOME of all the micekings: They fight with everyone, *ATTACK* drekars for no reason, and are always **hunting** for treasure, especially when it's not theirs to take!

Their village of **Feargard** is a scary place overlooking a gulf full of sharp rocks and **ferocious** sharks.

"I want to go home!" I whined.

"Stop complaining, you **jellyfish**!" Olaf thundered.

"Maybe the alarm was for the **VİLEKİNGS** instead of the dragons," Thea guessed.

Why were the vilekings sailing in the waters off the coast of **Mouseborg**? What were they up to? It wasn't anything **good**, that's for sure!

"Let's follow them!" Olaf commanded.

So Olaf the Fearless turned *Bated Breath* around. We followed the vilekings' drekar to a HIDDEN cove, where we put down our anchor and disembarked. Then we crept down a narrow passage carved in some rocks. It led to the entrance of a DARK CAVE.

"Is this really a **GOOD IDEA**?" I whispered to Olaf. "What's our plan, Captain?"

"Plan?" he replied in surprise.

"What?!" I exclaimed. "You mean you **DRAGGED US** off our boat without a plan?"

Thea rolled her eyes at me.

"Don't be such a scaredy-mouseking, Geronimo!" she said. "I'm going in. Are the rest of you coming?"

I didn't want to wait at the cave entrance all a̶l̶o̶n̶e̶, so I followed. Everyone else did, too. My sister sure is a courageous MOUSEKING!

The cave was huge, humid, and very, very **DARK**.

"Look!" Thea **WHISPERED** triumphantly. "There, in the back! It's the finnbrew

90

barrels that were stolen from the Mouseborg WAREHOUSE!"

"So you've **found** us out!" a voice behind us roared. "Too bad for you! SO SAYS RATNOLF THE TERRIBLE!"

"**Sh-shame** on you!" I stammered in reply. "You stole our finnbrew!"

"**QUIET**, fool!" Ratnolf replied. "I'm the only one who gets to talk! Ah, I am really, really **terrible**!"

At those words, the other vilekings in the

RATNOLF THE TERRIBLE

He is the head of the vilekings of Feargard. He is mean and disrespectful, and the only thing he cares about is being the most terrible. You can recognize him by the gold rings in his ears and the patch on his eye (He can see fine without it, but he seems more terrible with it!).

I am really, really terrible!

cave repeated in unison:

"AH, RATNOLF THE TERRIBLE IS REALLY, REALLY TERRIBLE!"

"Tie these micekings to the rock in the cove!" Ratnolf ordered his henchmice. "That way they'll have to behave as we load the finnbrew onto our drekar and sail out of here. Ah, I'm really, really terrible!"

All the vilekings around him shouted:

"AH, RATNOLF THE TERRIBLE IS REALLY, REALLY TERRIBLE!"

"You'll never get away with this, you leftover sea-foam!" Olaf shouted as they tied us to the rock.

"Quiet, mouseking!" Ratnolf ordered.

As the vilekings loaded the drekar, we suffered under the SCORCHING sun.

It was very, very **HOT**!

But suddenly, the **DROPS** of sweat that were hanging from my whiskers turned **icy** with fright.

"Great groaning glaciers, no!" I cried. "Th-those are the —"

"Shhh!" Thea *SHUSHED* me. "Stop complaining and save your breath, Geronimo!"

"B-but, b-but," I continued, my whiskers trembling with **FEAR**. "The dra . . . the drag . . . **the dragons**!"

MICEKING MEAT, COOKED TO PERFECTION!

A pair of dragons was flying over the **MOUSEBORG** fjord. As they *approached* us, they sniffed the air.

"Do you **SSS**mell that *aroma*, Greenpepper?" one dragon hissed.

"Ye**SSS**, I **SSS**mell it, Bitter!" the other replied. "Miceking meat, **cooked** to perfection!"

The dragons had **long** talons and mouths full of ⌇⊟⍝⍀⊡ teeth.

"Look!" the first dragon cried. "It'**SSS** a grill full of miceking meat! What a deliciou**SSS** **SSS**nack!"

"Quick! Let'**SSS** gobble them up!" Greenpepper replied, smacking his tongue.

As soon as he saw the dragons, Ratnolf changed his orders.

"**Dragons in sight!**" he shouted to his crew. "Vilekings to the drekar! Hoist the anchor!"

The vilekings fled the cave, leaving the barrels of finnbrew behind.

"**SAVE YOUR FUUUUR!**"
"**RETREEEEAT!**"
"**HEAD BACK TO FEARGAAAARD!**"

Before we could move a WHISKER, the vilekings were back aboard their drekar.

"QUICK! Row faster!" Ratnolf urged them. "Let's get out of here!"

They left us there, **tied** to the rock and **roasting** like miceking shish kebabs! We were fried, finished, done for!

"What about us?" Bugsilda sounded worried.

"How will we **ESCAPE**, Uncle Geronimo?" Benjamin asked.

Crusty codfish! I didn't know what to do. So I looked at **THEA**, hoping she had thought of something. She was trying to untie herself, but with **NO** luck!

"I can't get free!" she squeaked.

Suddenly, a flame from one of the two dragons passed so close to me that it **SINGED** my whiskers.

I began to shake and tremble so much that the ropes around me loosened, and I was able to free one paw.

"Try to grab my whistle, Geronimo!" Thea said. "That way we can call for **HELP**!"

"But is it really a good idea to draw attention to ourselves?" I argued. "Wouldn't it be better to free ourselves and **RUN**?"

"Uncle G, just do what Aunt Thea says!" Benjamin and Bugsilda squeaked in unison.

So, shaking like a bowl of jellyfish, I grabbed the **BRASS WHISTLE** my sister wore around her neck and put it up to her lips. She blew it in the **nick of time**!

The two dragons had just landed in front of us, saliva **dripping** from their mouths.

Greenpepper looked me up and down, from the ends of my whiskers to the tip of my tail.

"Let'**SSS SSS**ee what the**SSS**e nice miceking**SSS** ta**SSS**te like," he hissed in my snout.

"They look **SSS**uperta**SSS**ty!" Bitter replied. "Can I have the one with the big tummy?"

"If you in**SSSiSSS**t," Greenpepper agreed. "But then tho**SSS**e two little one**SSS** count as one, and I get them both!"

This time there was no way out: We

were †ieD UP and surrounded by dragons with a weakness for roasted **miceking meat**.

Suddenly, a **sweet** song filled the air. A moment later, a sparkly blue dragon with turquoise eyes and a silver crown appeared in the sky.

I couldn't believe my eyes!

"It's **Sapphire**!" I shouted with glee.

REVENGE OF THE BLUE DRAGON!

As **Sapphire** distracted the other dragons, Thea whispered in my ear.

"I called for him with my whistle," she explained.

But of course! Sapphire is Thea's friend. He is the last descendant of the legendary **Blue Dragon** race. He is a kind and friendly dragon who saved us once before.

Sapphire flew closer to the other dragons.

"Our leader, **Gobbler the Putrid**, wa**sss** right!" Bitter hissed in surprise. "The Blue Dragon**sss** aren't *extinct*!"

"**SSS**o what do we do now?" Greenpepper **GROWLED**. "I'm **SSS**tarved!"

"Let'**SSS** leave the micekings to roa**SSS**t for a bit longer," Ritter suggested. "Meanwhile, let'**SSS** get rid of thi**SSS** pe**SSS**t!"

"Good **IDEA**!" Greenpepper replied. "They'll be even ta**SSS**tier in a few more minute**SSS**!"

The two dragons left us to **CHASE** Sapphire. But the **flying** skills of the Blue Dragons are **legendary**!

Sapphire avoided

SαPPHIRE

Sapphire is the last of the legendary Blue Dragons, a clan of peaceful and friendly creatures!

He is a champion flier, and he loves singing sweet songs. Most important, he is a vegetarian who defends the micekings against the evil meat-eating dragons! He lives in the Valley of the Blue Rainbow. It's a secret place, so don't tell anyone!

He's so quick . . .

Where did he go?

Ha, ha, ha!

every **FLAMING** breath Greenpepper and Bitter aimed at him. The three dragons **twisted** and turned in the sky in an amazing display of advanced flying maneuvers. I was so busy watching Sapphire that I forgot I had a **FREE PAW**!

"Geronimo, don't just stare into the sky like a FISH FILLET!" Thea yelled at me. "Quick! Loosen the ropes!"

I freed myself and then **FREED** Thea. Together, we *untied* the others.

Above us, the evil dragons swayed and panted as they tried to keep up with **Sapphire**. But he was *too quick* for them!

Benjamin and Bugsilda cheered.

"Yeah!" Benjamin cried. "That's how it's done!"

"Serves you right, you **SCALY SNOUTS**!" Bugsilda added.

We watched as Sapphire landed on one of the whale islands.

"Thi**SSS** i**SSS** our chance, Bitter!" Greenpepper grunted furiously. "Let'**SSS** defeat him once and for all!"

With that, the two dragons **DOVE** downward. Sapphire waited until they were close, then **TAPPED** the whale's back with his tail. The giant fin whale took off with a **splash**!

105

A powerful spray of water hit the dragons in their snouts. They **growled** furiously. Then they tried to land on the whale islands to regroup. But each time a dragon landed, a whale hit him with another spray of water.

Everyone knows dragons hate water: It washes away their sulfurous **stench**, soaks their wings, and gives them **terrible colds**!

"Aaah! Water!" Greenpepper roared.

"It'**SSS** di**SSS**gu**SSS**ting!" Bitter hissed. "Let'**SSS** get out of here!"

They flew off, **shrieking** and **sneezing** as they went.

When Sapphire landed on the rock next to us, Thea ran to hug him.

"Thank you, my friend," she said, smiling. "You **SAVED** us! I know you have to go back to the Valley of the Blue Rainbow, but first, here's a **THANK-YOU** gift!"

My sister took a **red apple** out of her bag and tossed it in the air.

Sapphire grabbed it happily before he flew off to his secret haven. I was ready for us to *return* home as well. I was about to board the drekar when Olaf the Fearless **grabbed me** by the tail.

"Where do you think you're going, codfish face?" he grunted. "First we need to reclaim the **STOLEN** finnbrew!"

THE MYSTERY
OF THE MISSING
FINNBREW

"We're not leaving until we've loaded up all the barrels of finnbrew!" Olaf said decisively.

"You mean every single one?" I asked.

"That's right — from the first to the last, you smarty-mouseking!" Olaf replied.

Great groaning glaciers! Those barrels were so heavy! Resigned, I began to roll the finnbrew barrels toward our drekar, one by one. Meanwhile, the little micekings explored the cave.

"Uncle Geronimo! Aunt Thea!" Benjamin exclaimed suddenly.

"Look!" Bugsilda said, pointing. "It's a SECRET PASSAGE!"

109

Behind the barrels was a narrow, **DARK** tunnel. Courageous Thea entered immediately, **FOLLOWED** by the little micekings.

I hesitated until Olaf gave me a **SHOVE**. "Get going, *smarty-mouseking*!" he squeaked. "You're worse than a mussel that's stuck in mud!"

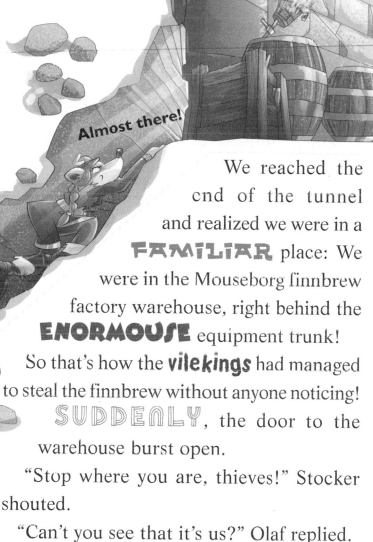

Almost there!

We reached the end of the tunnel and realized we were in a **FAMILIAR** place: We were in the Mouseborg finnbrew factory warehouse, right behind the **ENORMOUSE** equipment trunk!

So that's how the **vilekings** had managed to steal the finnbrew without anyone noticing! **SUDDENLY**, the door to the warehouse burst open.

"Stop where you are, thieves!" Stocker shouted.

"Can't you see that it's us?" Olaf replied.

"We figured out who **STOLE** the finnbrew!" Thea announced. "We must tell Sven!"

When we reached him, the village chief was **declaring** the winner of the **Famouse Fjord Race**.

"The winning drekar is . . . the *Cyclone Prince!*" Sven shouted.

All the micekings applauded except Ratilde and her crew.

"That fluke face wasn't a **GOOD** sportsmouse!" she accused Scowl. "He doesn't deserve to win!"

"It's true," Thora agreed. "When we were in trouble, he took off without helping us. But the *Bated Breath* offered to save our crew!"

Sven was SILENT for a moment before he squeaked again.

"Since Snarl and his crew weren't good sportsmice, the victory goes to Ratilde's team!"

Snarl stormed off, **FURIOUS**, while Ratilde and her crew CELEBRATED.

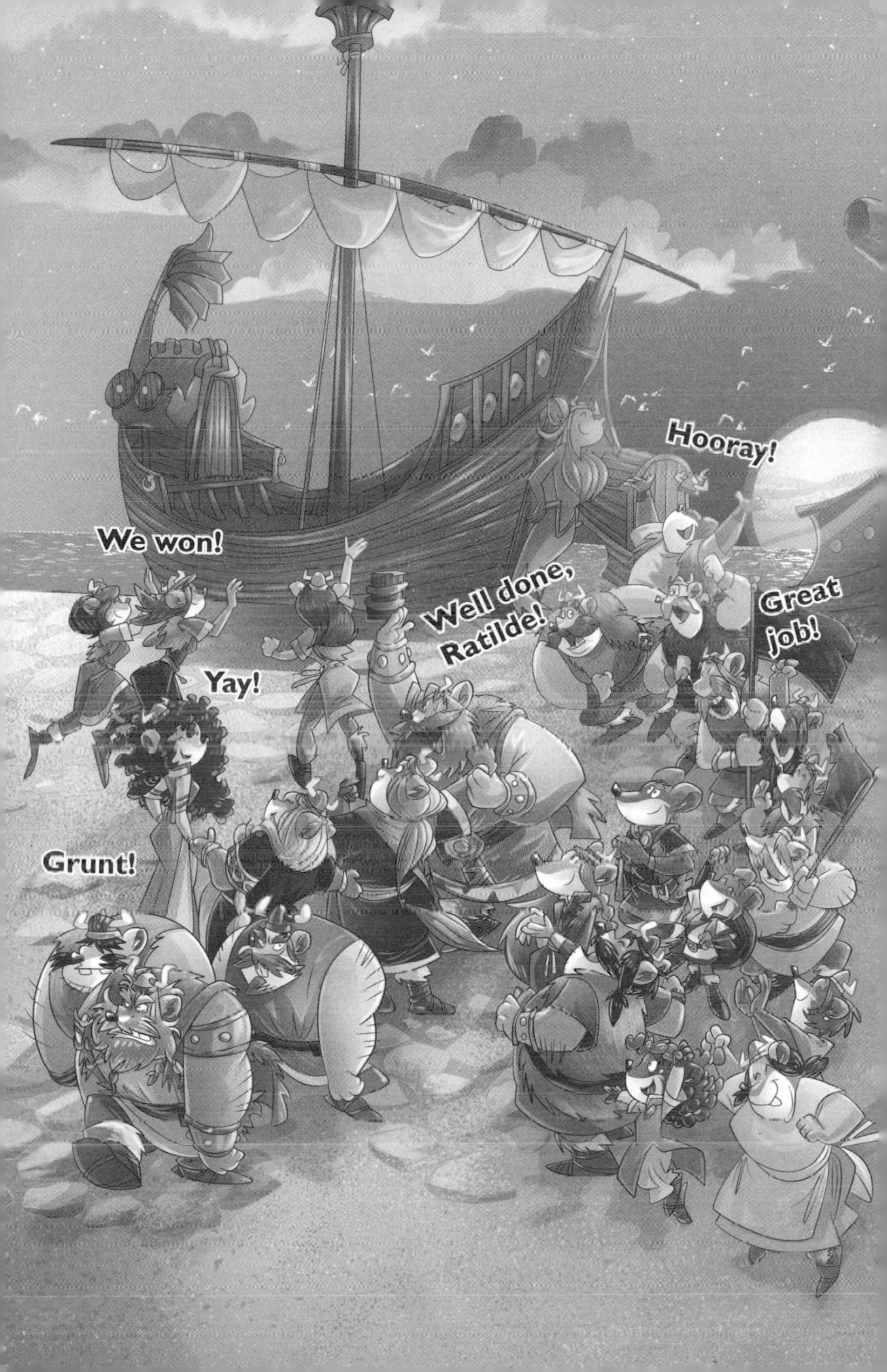
Hooray!
We won!
Well done, Ratilde!
Great job!
Yay!
Grunt!

"I'm sorry about the race, Captain," I told Olaf. "I know how much you wanted to **win!**"

"Ah, you know what I say, smarty-mouseking," Olaf replied. "My **old** and **crusty** *Bated Breath* is the best drekar there is. I don't need another one!"

At that moment, Sven caught sight of me.

"Geronimo!" he thundered. "Your team was the *last* to arrive!"

"But we solved the mystery of the missing finnbrew," Olaf explained.

After he heard our story, **SVEN THE SHOUTER** got back up on the stage.

"Attention, micekings!" he shouted. "In honor of the victors, and to celebrate the return of our finnbrew . . . gloog for everyone!"

"Hooray!" shouted the micekings of Mouseborg.

During the banquet, Thora approached me.

"Thank you for helping us, Geronimo," she said. "You are really a COURAGEOUS mouseking!" I turned **RED** with embarrassment. Then I pulled my WHISKERS to make sure I wasn't having another dream. It wasn't just my friends and family who believed in me — Thora did, too! With their help, I knew someday I would earn my very own **miceking helmet**!

BUT THAT'S ANOTHER MICEKING STORY FOR ANOTHER DAY!

Want to read the next adventure of the micekings? I can't wait to tell you all about it!

PULL THE DRAGON'S TOOTH!

Miceking chief Sven the Shouter has a new goal: to transform smarty-mouse Geronimo Stiltonord into a true macho mouseking. Geronimo must undergo special training, leading up to a terrifying final test: pulling a tooth from a dragon's mouth! Shivering squids! Will he ever earn a miceking helmet?

Don't miss the first adventure of the micekings, either!

Be sure to read all my fabumouse adventures!

#1 Lost Treasure of the Emerald Eye

#2 The Curse of the Cheese Pyramid

#3 Cat and Mouse in a Haunted House

#4 I'm Too Fond of My Fur!

#5 Four Mice Deep in the Jungle

#6 Paws Off, Cheddarface!

#7 Red Pizzas for a Blue Count

#8 Attack of the Bandit Cats

#9 A Fabumouse Vacation for Geronimo

#10 All Because of a Cup of Coffee

#11 It's Halloween, You 'Fraidy Mouse!

#12 Merry Christmas, Geronimo!

#13 The Phantom of the Subway

#14 The Temple of the Ruby of Fire

#15 The Mona Mousa Code

#16 A Cheese-Colored Camper

#17 Watch Your Whiskers, Stilton!

#18 Shipwreck on the Pirate Islands

#19 My Name Is Stilton, Geronimo Stilton

#20 Surf's Up, Geronimo!

#21 The Wild, Wild West

#22 The Secret of Cacklefur Castle

A Christmas Tale

#23 Valentine's Day Disaster

#24 Field Trip to Niagara Falls

#25 The Search for Sunken Treasure

#26 The Mummy with No Name

#27 The Christmas Toy Factory

#28 Wedding Crasher

#29 Down and Out Down Under

#30 The Mouse Island Marathon

#31 The Mysterious Cheese Thief

Christmas Catastrophe

#32 Valley of the Giant Skeletons

#33 Geronimo and the Gold Medal Mystery

#34 Geronimo Stilton, Secret Agent

#35 A Very Merry Christmas

#36 Geronimo's Valentine

#37 The Race Across America

#38 A Fabumouse School Adventure

#39 Singing Sensation

#40 The Karate Mouse

#41 Mighty Mount Kilimanjaro

#42 The Peculiar Pumpkin Thief

#43 I'm Not a Supermouse!

#44 The Giant
Diamond Robbery

#45 Save the White
Whale!

#46 The Haunted
Castle

#47 Run for the Hills,
Geronimo!

#48 The Mystery in
Venice

#49 The Way of
the Samurai

#50 This Hotel Is
Haunted!

#51 The Enormouse
Pearl Heist

#52 Mouse in Space!

#53 Rumble in
the Jungle

#54 Get into Gear,
Stilton!

#55 The Golden
Statue Plot

#56 Flight of the
Red Bandit

The Hunt for the
Golden Book

#57 The Stinky
Cheese Vacation

#58 The Super
Chef Contest

#59 Welcome to
Moldy Manor

The Hunt for the
Curious Cheese

#60 The Treasure of
Easter Island

#61 Mouse House
Hunter

#62 Mouse
Overboard!

The Hunt for the
Secret Papyrus

#63 The Cheese
Experiment

#64 Magical Mission

Don't miss any of my very special editions!

THE KINGDOM OF FANTASY

THE QUEST FOR PARADISE:
THE RETURN TO THE KINGDOM OF FANTASY

THE AMAZING VOYAGE:
THE THIRD ADVENTURE IN THE KINGDOM OF FANTASY

THE DRAGON PROPHECY:
THE FOURTH ADVENTURE IN THE KINGDOM OF FANTASY

THE VOLCANO OF FIRE:
THE FIFTH ADVENTURE IN THE KINGDOM OF FANTASY

THE SEARCH OR TREASURE:
HE SIXTH ADVENTURE IN THE KINGDOM OF FANTASY

THE ENCHANTED CHARMS:
THE SEVENTH ADVENTURE IN THE KINGDOM OF FANTASY

THE PHOENIX OF DESTINY:
AN EPIC KINGDOM OF FANTASY ADVENTURE

THE HOUR OF MAGIC:
THE EIGHTH ADVENTURE IN THE KINGDOM OF FANTASY

THE WIZARD'S WAND:
THE NINTH ADVENTURE IN THE KINGDOM OF FANTASY

THE JOURNEY THROUGH TIME

BACK IN TIME:
THE SECOND JOURNEY THROUGH TIME

THE RACE AGAINST TIME
THE THIRD JOURNEY THROUGH TIME

Dear mouse friends, thanks for reading,

and good-bye until the next book!